Ouch!

A Tale from Grimm Retold by Natalie Babbitt

Illustrated by

Fred Marcellino

MICHAEL DI CAPUA BOOKS / HARPER COLLINS PUBLISHERS

There was a baby boy born once with a birthmark shaped like a crown. "No question about it," said the local fortune-teller. "When he grows up, he's going to marry a princess." This was happy news to a family that was nobody special, but not happy news to the King. When he heard about it, he was up all night growling. What! *His* princess, who'd just been born herself? He would never let her marry nobody special.

So the King dressed up like someone else and rode out to the village where the family lived. "I hear this baby boy of yours is going to marry a princess someday," he said to the mother and father. And they told him it was true.

"Well," said the King, "you'd better give him to me. I'll raise him properly so he'll know how to act when the time comes." This struck the baby's parents as sensible, and anyway, the King gave them gold to seal the bargain. So the King took the baby away in a box, and when he came to a river, he threw the box into the water. "That takes care of that," he said to himself, and rode home smiling.

However, the box didn't sink to the bottom. Instead, it floated along for miles and at last bumped into a mill-dam. Here it was discovered by the miller, who fished it out, and when he and his wife opened it up, there was the baby, cooing happily.

Well, they were tickled pink because they had no children. They named the baby Marco, just right for such a voyager, and vowed to raise him as their very own. They might have named him Rex, which means "king," if they'd known what his future was to be, but of course they had no way of knowing.

Sixteen years went by with Marco grown up tall and sweet and full of confidence, which he was going to need, for here came the King one day, and right away he noticed Marco.

"That's a fine boy you've got there," he told the miller.

"Thank you, Sire," said the miller. "The fact is, we found him in a box on the river sixteen years ago and raised him as our very own."

The King saw the truth at once. But he hid his rage and said, "Tell him to take a message to the Queen." And then he wrote a letter: "Get rid of this boy. He's bad luck and I want him dead." And he sealed it and gave it to Marco, who started out for the castle.

Marco was full of confidence, yes, but in spite of that, he lost his way going through a forest. And after wandering about till it was nighttime, he lay down at last under a tree and went to sleep.

Then along came four bandit brothers, by the glow of a swaying lantern, who thought there must be money in Marco's pouch. They sneaked it off without waking him up, but the only thing they found inside was the King's letter, which of course they proceeded to read. "Come," said the oldest brother, "we can have some fun with this!"

So they wrote a new letter with new instructions: "Here is the boy I've chosen to marry the Princess. Don't wait—have the wedding now." They had a good laugh about it as they tiptoed away, and next day Marco, none the wiser, went on to the castle. The Queen read the letter and was happy to do what it said, for Marco and the Princess had fallen in love at first sight.

So the two were married, with plenty of joy and noise,

and that should have been the end of it. But it wasn't.

Once again, it was lucky that Marco was so full of confidence because he was going to need it now more than ever. The King came home in the middle of things and when he saw what had happened, he was furious. But all at once he had an idea. "Before you can settle in with my daughter," he said to Marco, "you'll have to go down to Hell and bring me three golden hairs from the Devil's head." And he grinned because he was sure the Devil would never let Marco come back.

But Marco said, "I can do that." And he kissed the Princess good-bye and started on his journey.

It was a long, long way, but Marco kept at it till at last he saw, far in the distance, the river that flows round the rim of Hell. And another hour brought him to its very banks, where he found a ferryman with a boat. "Can you take me across?" he asked.

"I'll take you," said the ferryman, "but not till you tell me how I can stop this endless backing and forthing. It's boring me to death."

"I'll find the answer," said Marco, "and I promise I'll report it

when I've finished with what I have to do."

So the ferryman, having no choice but to put his trust in this tall, sweet, confident boy, took him into the boat and poled him across the river.

Oh, what a scene of gloom and ruin Hell turned out to be!

It was easy to see why no one was anxious to go there.

Marco went down anyway and soon arrived at a hall where an old woman sat by a fire. He asked for the Devil, but she shook her head. "He's out, thank goodness," she said, "or he'd snap your nose off. I should know. I'm his grandmother."

Then Marco told her what he needed, but she said, "He wouldn't like losing any golden hairs. There aren't that many left from the old days in Heaven."

"But I have to have three," said Marco, "or else I lose the Princess."

"Dear me!" she said. "We can't let that happen. I'll see what I can do."

"And," he added, "one thing more. The ferryman wants to know how to stop being the ferryman."

"I'll find a way to ask," she said. "But you stay out of sight." And she worked a spell to make him so tiny he could have hidden in a shoe.

At suppertime the Devil came home, and right away he sniffed and made a face. "There's a man somewhere about," he said. "I can smell him."

"What rubbish," said his grandmother. "There's no one here. Sit down and eat."

So the Devil did as he was told, and afterward stretched out with his head in his grandmother's lap.

Then, when he dozed off, she found the golden hairs and yanked them out.

"Ouch!" he cried, waking up.

"I'm sorry," she said. "I went to sleep myself and dreamed I pulled the ferryman's hair. He was nagging me to do his job for him."

"That was a silly dream," said the Devil. "All he had to do was put the pole in your hand. Then it would stick to you, you see, so you'd have to take over his job, like it or not."

"Well, well," she said. "Imagine such a thing!"

The Devil went back to sleep after that and slept all night with no more rude disturbances.

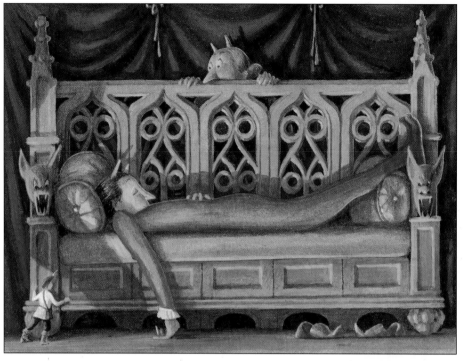

In the morning, when he'd once again gone off to tend to business, his grandmother changed Marco back to normal size and gave him the three golden hairs. And she told him the secret of the ferryman's job. Then, for good measure, she gave him a chest of coins and jewels.

"Here is a present for the Princess," she said to Marco. "May I never see the two of you in Hell."

Marco thanked her for this and for all she had done to help him, and she sent him on his way.

At the river, the ferryman was waiting. "Good news," said Marco. "To get rid of this job, just hand the pole to someone else."

"As easy as that?" said the ferryman. "Here, then—you take it."

"Oh, no, not me," said Marco with a laugh.

"Then whoever comes next will have a new life's work," said the ferryman. "I'll see to that!"

So they went back across the river, where Marco untied his donkey and hurried away to the castle.

ell, my sweet!" he said to the Princess. "See what I have for you!" And he opened the chest of coins and jewels. "Oh, and by the way," he said to the King, "here are the golden hairs you wanted."

But the King ignored the hairs. "Where did you get that treasure?" he demanded.

"Why," said Marco, "a ferryman took me across a river and there it was on the other side."

"Oho!" said the King. "Maybe there's more just sitting there!"

"Maybe," said Marco. "Why don't you go and see?"

So the King dashed off towards Hell. And he never came back.

Marco took over the job of being king, and he and the Princess

lived happily ever after. In fact, everyone was happy. Almost.

For the King, a king no more, now had the job of taking people back and forth, back and forth across the river that flows round the rim of Hell, with no idea at all how to stop.